POKÉMON™

STORYBOOK TREASURY

A Random House PICTUREBACK® Book

Random House 🏠 New York

Book design by John Sazaklis

© 2018 The Pokémon Company International. © 1995–2018 Nintendo / Creatures Inc. / GAME FREAK Inc. TM, ®, and character names are trademarks of Nintendo. Published in the United States by Random House Children's Books, a division of Penguin Random House LLC, 1745 Broadway, New York, NY 10019, and in Canada by Penguin Random House Canada Limited, Toronto. These stories were originally published separately in different form by Random House Books for Young Readers as *Ash & Pikachu: Alola Region / Team Rocket: Alola Region* in 2017, *Famous Friends & Foes* in 2017, and *Favorite First Friends!* in 2018. Pictureback, Random House, and the Random House colophon are registered trademarks of Penguin Random House LLC.
rhcbooks.com
ISBN 978-1-5247-7259-8
MANUFACTURED IN CHINA
10 9 8 7 6 5 4 3 2 1

CONTENTS

POKÉMON™

ASH & PIKACHU: ALOLA REGION

BY RACHEL CHLEBOWSKI

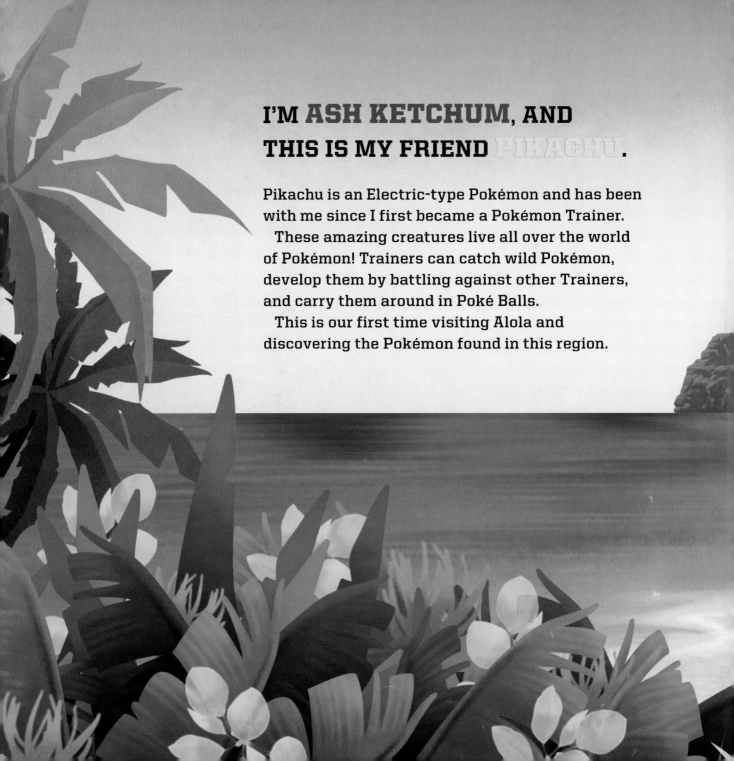

I'M **ASH KETCHUM**, AND THIS IS MY FRIEND PIKACHU.

Pikachu is an Electric-type Pokémon and has been with me since I first became a Pokémon Trainer.

These amazing creatures live all over the world of Pokémon! Trainers can catch wild Pokémon, develop them by battling against other Trainers, and carry them around in Poké Balls.

This is our first time visiting Alola and discovering the Pokémon found in this region.

ROWLET, LITTEN, and **POPPLIO** are three Pokémon you are likely to meet early in your adventures in Alola. There are many different types of Pokémon in the world—eighteen have been discovered so far! Pokémon enjoy the chance to gain experience by battling other Pokémon!

EEVEE is amazingly adaptive, with eight different Pokémon known to evolve from it due to its unstable genetic structure.

YUNGOOS has sharp teeth and a vast appetite. It can spend all day looking for food and will eat just about anything, but will fall asleep as soon as the sun sets.

ROWLET is a Grass- and Flying-type Pokémon that can sneak up on foes with its silent flight and flurry of kicking attacks! **LITTEN** prefers to be alone and doesn't show emotion easily. This Pokémon can attack with fiery fur balls!

POPPLIO is a hardworking Pokémon that can create water bubbles from its nose to use in battle!
BOUNSWEET smells good enough to eat and produces a sweet liquid that makes a yummy treat when watered down.

LYCANROC has two forms, both of which have rocky manes that are useful in battle. When raised well by its Trainer, Lycanroc's Midday Form makes a fiercely loyal companion.

Lycanroc in its Midnight Form will attack with its crushing headbutts.

8

ROCKRUFF is a Rock-type Pokémon that may evolve into either form of Lycanroc!

FUN FACT:
Rockruff is a friendly Pokémon. Professor Kukui at the Alola Pokémon School has one!

Some Pokémon can evolve—and when they do, they become totally different! Pikachu evolves from **PICHU** and can evolve into **RAICHU**. All three are Electric types.

In Alola, Raichu are unlike Raichu found elsewhere.

ALOLAN RAICHU is an Electric- and Psychic-type Pokémon and can surf on its tail!

TOGEDEMARU is not known to evolve. The spiny hairs on its back come in handy against foes and can attract lightning!

DITTO can change its shape into anything! It uses its transformation talent to befriend other Pokémon.

ALOLAN VULPIX was once known in Alola as Keokeo. It is an Ice-type Pokémon that uses its six tails to create a spray of ice crystals to cool itself off when it gets too hot.

FUN FACT:
Vulpix evolves into Ninetales, and **ALOLAN NINETALES** is an Ice- and Fairy-type Pokémon!

CLEFFA loves watching shooting stars streak through the night sky. Cleffa and its evolutions, CLEFAIRY and CLEFABLE, charm other Pokémon they meet. CUTIEFLY can sense the auras of flowers—and a floral aura in people, too. The flowers on COMFEY's vine release a calming fragrance. Adding these flowers to bathwater will make for a relaxing soak!

13

PIKIPEK can drill holes in trees for storing berries, used for both food and attacks. It evolves into TRUMBEAK, which can store berries in its beak. Trumbeak evolves into TOUCANNON, which can shoot burning seeds from its heated beak!

GRUBBIN uses its strong jaws to scrape away tree bark so it can eat the sap. When Grubbin evolves into **CHARJABUG**, it stores the energy it gets from food as electricity!

VIKAVOLT, the final form, can stun its opponents with a powerful ZAP!

SOLGALEO is a Legendary Pokémon! When Solgaleo's third eye activates, it can depart for another world, where it is said to make its home.

FUN FACT:

Solgaleo radiates light that can wipe away the darkness of the world.

POKÉMON™

TEAM ROCKET: ALOLA REGION

BY
RACHEL
CHLEBOWSKI

DID SOMEONE ASK SOMETHING? We're here to find out!
Noble answers are what we're about!

The radiant beauty of flowers and moon hides in shame.
A single flower of evil in this fleeting world: **JESSIE**!

The nobly heroic man of our times! The master of darkness
fighting back against a tragic world! It's **JAMES**.

We're here in the Alola region to catch a certain **PIKACHU**—
and some Alolan Pokémon, too!

It's all for one and one for all! A glittering dark star that always shines bright! Dig it while **MEOWTH** takes flight! WOBBUFFET!

Oh, no! TEAM ROCKET is in Alola, too? They have a talking Meowth that assists them in scamming people. MEOWTH can't usually speak—but this one does! They also travel with a WOBBUFFET, a Psychic-type Pokémon capable of patiently enduring any attack—except one on its tail!

Jessie and James keep trying to steal other people's Pokémon! Team Rocket has been trying to take PIKACHU ever since they lost in battle to Pikachu back in the Kanto region.

GUMSHOOS is the evolved form of **YUNGOOS**. It is an amazingly patient Pokémon when it's staking out foes.

ALOLAN RATICATE is the evolved form of Alolan Rattata. In Alola, each Raticate leads a group of Rattata to find—and fight over—food.

SALANDIT is known to make its home near volcanoes and dry places. Don't get too close! It blasts a poisonous gas in its enemies' faces!

MUDBRAY loves to play in the mud! The mud on its hooves keeps it from slipping and allows it to run faster.

FUN FACT:

MUDBRAY evolves into **MUDSDALE.**

SABLEYE loves shiny gemstones. Legend has it that this Pokémon can steal people's spirits!

WEAVILE often battles with the cold-dwelling Vulpix and Sandshrew. It carves up rocks and trees with its sharp claws to communicate with others of its kind.

ALOLAN SANDSHREW lives on snowy mountains. It is very good at using its shell to slide across the ice.

Ground-type SANDSHREW, seen elsewhere, can roll its body into a ball, but ALOLAN SANDSHREW cannot.

LUCARIO can sense auras and control them. It can tell if a person or Pokémon is feeling happy or sad if they are standing within a half-mile radius!

KLEFKI loves to collect keys. If you're always losing your keys, a Klefki might be responsible—it sometimes swipes keys from people's houses!

Watch out for **BEWEAR**! It might seem friendly, but its bone-crushing hugs can be very dangerous!

FUN FACT:
STUFFUL is the adorable Flailing Pokémon before it evolves into **BEWEAR**!

BRUXISH has psychic powers that cause the grating sound of its gnashing teeth to echo in its enemies' ears. Don't let its enticing grin fool you!

METANG, the Iron Claw Pokémon, loves magnetic minerals and has the psychic power of two Beldum!

LYCANROC has two forms. Its Midday Form is fiercely loyal when raised by a good Trainer who treats it well. Its Midnight Form is recklessly brave, attacking with no regard for its own safety.

GOOMY is somewhat small for a Dragon-type Pokémon. Its slimy covering protects it from attacks!

Created from a child's mound of sand, SANDYGAST can take control of anyone who puts a hand in its mouth!

Is that a **PIKACHU**? No, it's a MIMIKYU! No one knows what it looks like underneath its costume, but apparently, the sight of its true appearance is terrifying—and even dangerous!

Mimikyu hides under an old rag so it can get closer to people and other Pokémon.

LUNALA is one of Alola's Legendary Pokémon, said to make its home in another world! It has wings that soak up the light, plunging the brightest day into darkness.

POKÉMON™

FAMOUS FRIENDS & FOES

BY
RACHEL
CHLEBOWSKI

WELCOME TO THE WORLD OF **POKÉMON**!

Pokémon Trainers can catch these incredible creatures in the wild and train them in battle to be the very best. Trainers just starting out in the Kanto region are likely to meet one of these three Pokémon early in their journey:

BULBASAUR is a Grass- and Poison-type Pokémon with a seed on its back. While napping, its seed absorbs sunlight and grows.

CHARMANDER is a Fire-type Pokémon. The flame on the tip of its tail indicates how it is feeling—if it flares up in a fury, watch out!

SQUIRTLE's shell protects it in battle. Its round shape and grooved surface allow the Pokémon to swim fast!

Some Pokémon can evolve into entirely different Pokémon.
When Bulbasaur evolves into **IVYSAUR**, the seed turns into a bud
on Ivysaur's back. Ivysaur has stronger legs to support the bud's weight.
Charmander evolves into **CHARMELEON**. When it becomes aggressive
against a foe, the flame at the end of its tail turns bluish white.
WARTORTLE is the evolved form of Squirtle. Wartortle's tail is large
and covered with thick fur that darkens in color as it gets older.

Ivysaur evolves into **VENUSAUR**. The large flower on its back is said to take on rich colors if it gets plenty of sunlight. It also has a soothing aroma.

When Charmeleon evolves into **CHARIZARD**, it seeks out worthy opponents and only breathes fire against these stronger foes.

Wartortle evolves into **BLASTOISE**. The waterspouts sticking out of its shell can hit their target from amazing distances!

JIGGLYPUFF can inflate its body like a balloon and sing at the right wavelength to make its opponent fall asleep. It can keep singing until everyone listening falls asleep!

DITTO is the Transform Pokémon. It can change its shape to resemble almost anything! It often uses this skill to try to befriend other Pokémon.

PIKACHU is an Electric-type Pokémon that stores electricity in its body. It releases that energy regularly to maintain good health. It evolves from **PICHU**. Pikachu evolves into **RAICHU**. This Pokémon can unleash so much electricity that it can defeat a larger foe with a single shock!

In the Alola region, Pikachu evolves into ALOLAN RAICHU.
Raichu is thought to look different in Alola because of what it eats.
Alolan Raichu can use its psychic power to surf on its tail.

VULPIX is a Fire-type Pokémon that is beloved for its fur and its multiple tails, which keep splitting as it grows.

The **ALOLAN VULPIX** is an Ice-type Pokémon. If it gets too hot, its six tails can create a spray of ice crystals to cool itself off.

44

Vulpix evolves into **NINETALES**, a Pokémon that can live for a thousand years. Myths say it was created when nine saints merged into a single being. The **ALOLAN NINETALES** is an Ice- and Fairy-type Pokémon. It is usually gentle, but when angered, it can freeze its enemies in their tracks.

ZUBAT spends its days sleeping in caves and uses ultrasonic waves to sense its environment. When Zubat evolves into GOLBAT, it develops eyes to see and uses its hollow fangs to suck blood. Sometimes it eats so much that it can't fly afterward!

CROBAT, the evolved form of Golbat, is a master of stealth and speed. Its hind legs have become an extra pair of wings!

GASTLY's presence can cause lights to flicker in the abandoned buildings it likes to lurk in. Though it is hard to see, this Pokémon gives off a delicately sweet scent.

Gastly evolves into **HAUNTER**. Haunter's lick can steal your life energy! It prefers to live in darkness and avoids city lights. **GENGAR** is the evolved form of Haunter, and brings an unexplainable chill to the air. Its mixed-up idea of friendship has led it to attack humans in an attempt to become friends.

49

MAGIKARP's habit of splashing about recklessly leaves it open to attack. Though it's not the strongest fighter in battle, it does exist in huge numbers.

When Magikarp evolves into **GYARADOS**, it grows about ten times larger! Gyarados has a notorious temper and an aptitude for destruction.

LAPRAS has a lovely singing voice. Friendly and intelligent, this Pokémon is often used for transportation on water.

SNORLAX's massive body needs about 900 pounds of food every day. It can eat just about anything! If it falls asleep while eating, it will continue to eat in its sleep.

EEVEE is the Evolution Pokémon. Its unstable genetic structure enables it to evolve into eight different Pokémon, according to current studies.

ESPEON

VAPOREON

GLACEON

UMBREON

JOLTEON

LEAFEON

SYLVEON

FLAREON

55

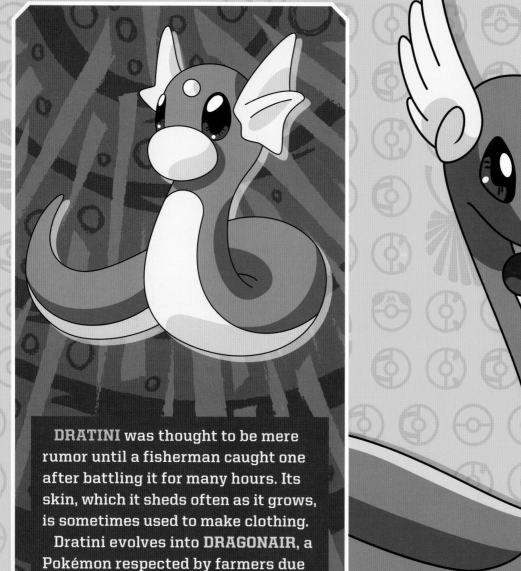

DRATINI was thought to be mere rumor until a fisherman caught one after battling it for many hours. Its skin, which it sheds often as it grows, is sometimes used to make clothing.

Dratini evolves into **DRAGONAIR**, a Pokémon respected by farmers due to its fabled ability to change the weather with the crystalline orbs on its body.

DRAGONITE evolves from Dragonair. Dragonite's wrath can be devastating. Luckily, this Pokémon has a kind and calm demeanor and is slow to anger.

MEW is said to possess the genetic makeup of all Pokémon. It can make itself invisible so that people will not notice it!

MEWTWO was created by genetic manipulation in an effort to re-create Mew. While this Pokémon is strong in both mind and body, it's made most dangerous by its lack of compassion.

The Pokémon world is an exciting place full of incredible, beloved Pokémon for you to discover. Train your Pokémon well as your journey continues!

Pokémon

FAVORITE FIRST FRIENDS!

BY C. J. NESTOR

ALOLA!

My name's **PROFESSOR KUKUI**, and I'm the Pokémon professor here on **ALOLA**! Alola is an island paradise, with sandy beaches and beautiful mountains. It's also chock-full of Pokémon!

Trainers enjoy the sun, explore the land, and collect and battle all the Pokémon we have in Alola!

Each region in the Pokémon world has its own three first-partner Pokémon that are Grass-type, Fire-type, and Water-type Pokémon. Nearly all young Trainers choose one of these Pokémon to accompany them on their first adventures!

Trainers who start their adventures in the **KANTO** region can choose
between the Grass-type **BULBASAUR**, the Fire-type **CHARMANDER**,
or the Water-type **SQUIRTLE** as their first-partner Pokémon!

BULBASAUR stores a seed in the large bulb on its back.
As it gathers sunlight, the seed on its back grows. I wonder
what happens when the seed gets really large!

Watch out for the flame on **CHARMANDER**'s tail!
When this Pokémon gets fired up, its tail burns
bright and hot. I bet that comes in handy during
Pokémon battles!

Check out the shell on **SQUIRTLE**! Its smooth surface lets
Squirtle swim at high speeds and protects it from attacks.
That strong defense makes it really tough in battle.

Have you heard of **JOHTO**? Trainers who start their
journey here pick between the Grass-type **CHIKORITA**,
the Fire-type **CYNDAQUIL**, or the Water-type **TOTODILE!**

CHIKORITA is a very friendly Pokémon. The leaf on its head smells sweet and makes everyone feel calm and happy. But when in battle, watch out, because this Pokémon can be as fierce as it is friendly!

When CYNDAQUIL is ready to fight, the fire on its back flares up, protecting it. But when it's sleepy, Cyndaquil's flames are small and sputter fitfully.

Trainers who choose **TOTODILE** as their partner are in for a good time! This playful little Pokémon will show affection, but watch out for its bite. Its jaws are very powerful, and sometimes it doesn't know its own strength!

Trainers from the **HOENN** region won't see any of those previously discovered first-partner Pokémon. Instead, they get their choice of the Grass-type **TREECKO**, the Fire-type **TORCHIC**, or the Water-type **MUDKIP**!

TREECKO has a thick tail, but what you really have to watch out for are its feet. It uses tiny hooks on its feet to climb trees and can attack from above. Look out below!

TORCHIC seems like a perfect cuddle buddy, with its soft feathers and inner fire. But this little Pokémon can produce flames so hot, they will leave its foes scorched black.

MUDKIP is really cute with all those fins, but they don't just look good. They also let Mudkip sense movement in the water and air around it, so it knows what's happening without opening its eyes.

Trainers who start their adventures in the **SINNOH** region normally choose between the Grass-type TURTWIG, the Fire-type CHIMCHAR, or the Water-type PIPLUP.

TURTWIG has a shell, but it's nothing like Squirtle's. This Pokémon's shell is made of hard-packed soil. Turtwig's whole body absorbs sunlight and water for energy.

CHIMCHAR has a flame on its back that flickers if it isn't feeling well. However, Chimchar's flame never goes out, even in the rain. Amazing!

PIPLUP are often stubborn and won't listen to their Trainers. However, if you work really hard, you'll be friends for life with the Penguin Pokémon!

Trainers who start their adventures in the **UNOVA** region are likely to choose between the Grass-type SNIVY, the Fire-type TEPIG, or the Water-type OSHAWOTT.

SNIVY loves the sun. Sunlight makes its movements swifter. It uses vines better than you use your hands, so keep an eye out for it where you least expect!

Trainers who want **TEPIG** as their first companion should like well-done food! This little Pokémon shoots fireballs out of its nose to roast berries to eat.

OSHAWOTT is a fierce Pokémon. The scalchop on its stomach isn't just for breaking open hard berries; this shell is also a sharp weapon!

The first-partner Pokémon unique to the **KALOS** region are the Grass-type **CHESPIN**, the Fire-type **FENNEKIN**, and the Water-type **FROAKIE!**

Trainers need to be careful if **CHESPIN** is their first-partner Pokémon. The quills on its head are soft, but become sharp enough to pierce rock! Trainers should keep their Chespin relaxed and happy before patting its head.

Watch out for the powerful Fire-type **FENNEKIN**! This Pokémon's cute
ears are actually a vent for the superheated air inside its body. Youch!

FROAKIE's bubbles protect its sensitive skin from damage. This makes Froakie tough to beat!

Of course, some Trainers start their adventures right here in Alola!
Trainers beginning in Alola get their choice of the Grass-type
ROWLET, the Fire-type **LITTEN**, or the Water-type **POPPLIO**!

ROWLET spends most of its day soaking up sunlight. It uses the energy it stores during the day to be more active at night. In battle, Rowlet will fly up to its foes and unleash a flurry of kicking attacks, so watch out!

When **LITTEN** grooms itself, it stores extra fur inside its stomach. To attack, it coughs up the fur and sets it on fire!

POPPLIO is a hardworking Pokémon, and it's always fun to have around. It blows bubbles out its nose and puts in lots of practice so it can use these as a weapon in battle!

Each of these first partner Pokémon can grow stronger and evolve into more-powerful Pokémon, like these evolutions of the Alola partners!

TORRACAT
Type: Fire

BRIONNE
Type: Water

DARTRIX
Type: Grass-Flying

DECIDUEYE
Type: Grass-Ghost

Each Pokémon has its own strengths, weaknesses, and abilities. To learn more about them, you know what to do!

PRIMARINA
Type: Water-Fairy

INCINEROAR
Type: Fire-Dark